Cover : Larisa KAZAKOVA

FACES

From the same author :

(E-books & version papier)

- Somewhere in Vladivostok
- Harcèlement (éd. BOD)
- Harassment (éd. BOD)
- Acoso (éd. BOD)
- Neith (La mystérieuse Nubienne) (éd. BOD)
- The Nubian (The mysterious Neith) (éd. BOD)
- Les macarons (éd. BOD)
- La veuve PLYNN (éd. BOD)
- Instants ultimes (éd. BOD)
- Que dire de plus ? (éd. BOD)
- Cousine ! (éd. BOD)
- Tu n'es pas la femme de l'homme
    que je suis (éd BOD)
- The day after in London (éd BOD)
- Londres : le jour d'après (éd BOD)
- Ma dernière nuit en Sibérie (éd BOD)
- My last night in Siberia (éd BOD)
- Facettes (éd BOD)

(www.bod.fr)

FACES

« ... *The encounter, is the adventure by which the subject comes out of himself to return to him, grown up or troubled* ... »

Leslie Morel

F A C E S

Thoughts.

6 *FACES*

At the beginning ….

It doesn't matter if it's a man or a woman you meet on this street, on this boulevard, in this commuter train, in an airport or in this square, in the middle of the day, a little by chance, that day while you were in your thoughts, relaxed or a bit concerned, in a hurry or nonchalant, loitering according to your mood.

Ordinary event in itself.

Two individuals driven by the same dynamic, each coming to meet the other, ignoring the existence of one and the other until this precise moment when, inexorably, two universes interpenetrate thus forming this private bubble whose existence will be limited in time (the time of the crossing), and in which, everything that has passed from beginning to end, will be irreversible.

Two singular universes, conveying pasts with disparate colors and smells or in perfect harmony, allowing to identify points of intersection, the result of pure chance or the illustration of a paradox (these two about to cross, having nothing in common), in no way foreshadowing what some might describe as "beautiful encounter" by comparing these two universes accidentally brought together.

In this particular context, suddenly, without knowing why, among the hundred faces, the look of a person catches yours to the point of attracting your attention.
What could push us to accept against all odds

this visual encounter and let us deliberately lock ourselves into this captivating and mysterious private bubble, a bubble whose lifespan will depend on the rhythm printed by our steps forwarding towards each other until the fateful moment of the crossing?

At first glance, nothing.

For how can we not feel free in a public space in which the very principle of our freedom is inalienable?

As if, against our will, our gaze is suddenly locked on a face met for the first time, and which in first analysis, does not present any of the peculiarities of the standards that might move us.

So, for the few meters to go before crossing the other, we are embarked in this bubble for a journey to the unknown to discover the other, ready to penetrate a universe unknown to us a few seconds earlier.

Successively, like a kaleidoscope turning on itself in front of a bright point, thus delivering alternately the multicolored facets of this mosaic of ethnicities, appear before us, randomly, Zorah, Pietro, Fatoumata, Edwige, Thierry, Pascaline, Lara, Ahmed, Lucie, Meryem, and many others who would not have managed to captivate us.

ZORAH

About thirty years old, not very tall, long hair frizzing ebony color, tied like a ponytail by means of a black velvet ribbon, thin pearly pink lips, dark grey pants, a parma colored blouse, a light grey blazer, red ballerinas.

Taking advantage of her meridian break, this newly named children's judge strolls through this tree-lined and flowery park.

Despite a very important workload and overwhelming responsibilities, Zorah imposes herself daily, this moment of relaxation allowing her to empty her mind, and try to regain a necessary serenity (the afternoon promising to be tiring), through this walk in this green environment, reassuring, and soothing.

Tough morning.

A dozen of extremely difficult judge appearances. Tense face-to-faces of multi-recidivist minors in front of her, Zorah, a children's judge, insulted, threatened with death, sometimes destitute in the face of what she considers to be the most unacceptable thing that can exist, when one attacks her authority as a judge, when one tramples on the function that is hers and for which she has made so many personal sacrifices to achieve it.

However, by choosing to study law in order to become a judge, she felt ready to face the world she was able to glimpse during her internships in the offices of the judges who welcomed her as an intern.

But, once being on her own (with her status as a judge for children, a status that commands her to observe the necessary distance to be in front of these minors, the judge and not the mother of two children whose education she supervises like milk on fire), she was a thousand places away to imagine the full extent of the consequences of this "social breakdown" at all levels of society

, starting with the parents's resignation in the face of their children's education.

Since the beginning of her career as a children's judge, she has always questioned herself about the purpose of her function.

If the function of the children's judge consists to intervene in the context of educational assistance to minors in danger, to educate and try minors accused of having committed crimes, what about the proven cases of parents who fail or even resign?

How can we proceed upstream to limit the production of all these serious cases of underage children adrift, in great perdition, out of bounds and to prevent the judge's office from becoming an spillway of all these social cases produced by the society that rejects them?

Would the methods taught in the schools of the judiciary be similar to those advocated in medical schools that teach students to identify a disease according to the symptoms and treat the said disease by focusing on the treatment of symptoms that are in fact ,(or mainly), visible signs or   the consequences of indirect dysfunctions?

Why is the global approach not doctrine? Why is it left out at the expense of the certainty that every deleterious social situation can never generate downstream all this not insignificant part of the society that populates the offices of judges?

The global approach which is also defined by the notion of an integral approach, "recognizes that a very important part of a person's difficulties is the product of human action that is foreign to him/her."

For her, applied to her chosen field, this foreign human action (having generated the dramatic consequences that she can see every day in her office), namely the resignation of parents in the face of their responsibility to educate and assist their minor children, is beyond doubt.

These parents, freeing themselves from their duties as educators by considering that, their mission as educators ends where that of the education system officially established and implemented by national education ministry, begin.

They feel "lighter" by getting rid of the most essential part of their responsibility on national education whose mission is not to instill the fundamental notions of respect, politeness, moral integrity, ...

Would they be coward by projecting on national education, the responsibility they refuse to assume, for their own children?

To their credit, how many parents are really available and armed to deal with the consequences of the desintegration of the society in which we live, a society in which nothing is in its place, nothing looks like (near or far) to the good old morality that once, populated (not so long ago) the spirit of men and women?

There was a time, when a beautiful car was parked on the street, it was the object of boundless admiration on the part of everyone.

FACES

People did not approach close to it, their hands almost behind their backs, for fear of touching it so as not to damage it.

Nowadays, at best its bodywork is scratched with a metal object, at worst, it is vandalized, stolen and burned.

What to do with desperate cases?

Invoke St-JUDE (the boss of lost causes) every morning before the start of the court appearances?

Doubt is allowed: the teaching of Christian charity is not part of the curriculum leading to the profession of magistrate.

So, apply the law in all its rigour by having the satisfaction of the duty accomplished by removing the imperfections of society and thus, eliminate all that exceeds and creates disorder?

To show leniency by thinking first of all, of the mother of the family (whose life is a permanent nightmare), totally damaged and overwhelmed by events, for who the severity of a judge's decision would only rekindle her pain of having failed in her role as a mother?

What about the institutions (of which the main one absent, is the parent's school) and the accompanying measures in the catalogue, made available to the children's judge, allowing her to "do her best"?

A second chance? A third chance? A fourth, a fifth? What happens next? How far would it take to attempt a rescue when all the lights have gone to scarlet red?

By nature, since the human brain cannot be reset in the same way as a computer's hard drive, how do we reprogram the multi-recidivist offender to put him back on the path to success and witness his redemption?

Zorah cannot escape to the constant questioning she carries within her, like a burden, even if, in this green environment embellished with birdsong, the serenity she shows and her detachment, can only last the time of a lunch break.

FACES

Personal notes

Personal notes

PIETRO

Looking surprisingly like Dick Rivers, Piétro is a mixed race son from a French mother and a Colombian father, a former professional cyclist who settled down in France since many years.

A family without problems of the Nantes region, in which harmony has gradually settled allowing to raise children in a healthy and serene family environment.

Piedtro is a part of a siblings, composed of two girls and three boys, a siblings in which he is in third position.

His coming into the world overshadowed the existence of the two sisters who preceded him, a birth that was properly welcomed by his status as the first boy born in the family.

Despite his status which opened him

exhorbiting rights as a child-king, Pietro was a model child, calm, obedient, avoiding bad dating, succeeding in his high school education that led him to pass and obtain a certificate of senior technician in the hotel industry, kitchen option.

Graduating after several internships in prestigious hotel establishments, he was able to reveal his secret dream of moving to the United States of America.

Everyone can easily imagine the long evenings discussion within the family.

A real earthquake.

He finally managed to convince his parents to let him go live his American dream.

In the secrecy of their bedroom, the parents continued many times late at night heated discussions about their son Pietro's project.

The father, (who knows well this almost obsessive feeling of leaving the family to settle elsewhere and to live the dream of another life), knows more than anyone how his son Pietro, (the first born male among his children), feels.

The mother, much more rooted in her land in Nantes, thinks that France, the great country of gastronomy, is large enough to allow her son to find his happiness in the exercise of his profession as a cook.

" ***No one is waiting for you there, my son.*** "

She repeated this advice many times to her son with tears in her eyes, with the secret hope of seeing him give up his plan to move to the United States.

In an attempt to calm his dear mother's concerns and to reiterate his determination to pursue his project, his favourite argument is the precept of St-Exupéry :

"***Make your life a dream, and a dream a reality.***"

Despite the profound meaning of this sentence against which there is almost nothing to object to, except the urgent need to remind everyone of the responsibility to lead our life in the best interests of our life, the wise pleas and advice coming from a cautious and worried mother, in the absence of the support of her husband who, on the contrary, pushes his son to go away to live his American dream , Piétro landed one autumn morning in New York, a city in which he knew vaguely a pastry buddy who had extolled to him the charms of this part of the world where, it seems, everyone lives and flourishes in abundance and joy.

His American dream could then begin without delay, since (always it seems) it's enough to bend over to amass fortune.

Three months later, he is back home, much to his mother's satisfaction and to his dad's despair.

His return home is the consequence of his sudden awareness that, it's better to avoid living under illusion in order not to get lost in disillusionment.

His mother's many pleas, the impreparation of his journey, the vagueness of his objectives, the vain expectations of something that is long to come or that will never begin, starting with obtaining the H-1B visa, finally have sowed doubt in his mind about his ability to remain in a country in which nobody expects him, a country in which, making a fortune is not exclusively a dream.

Knowing that doubt leads to wisdom (according to Henri-Frédéric Amiel), and that wisdom has the virtue of presenting illusion in its "best" profile in order to no longer delude and avoid continuing our path towards disillusionment, Piétro understood that there is no point in persisting in his will to make a fortune away from home and that it was time to mourn this dream which has inhabited his imagination for a while , depriving him of his discernment, forcing him to ignore his mother's wisdom.

When drowning is inevitable, and we have only the water that surrounds us to grab hold of us, can we reasonably judge that the fact to give up our desire to throw ourselves into the water, as a lack of courage or, on the contrary, to take it as an act of courage?

Personal notes

Personal notes

FATOUMATA

Fatoumata walks nonchalantly through the crowded aisles of the market in this popular district of Paris.

Her lips are painted an indigo blue. What makes her face characteristic.

Her return trip to Africa is near.

In order not to return empty-handed, she comes to collect the latest beauty products ordered by the women of her neighbourhood in her country, products that cost a real fortune in the local shops, with in addition, the risk of counterfeiting, causing serious health problems in the population, problems before which the authorities are powerless.

The most rich of them, use her services to find in Paris, these pots of cream having the vocation to lighten the color of the skin of face and body, these lotions for frizzy hair likely to make them silkier, etc … .

A true saleswoman who lives six months in Europe and six months in her home country.

Her profession obliges her to organize her life in this way, spending her time between two continents.

Fatoumta is a matchmaker.

The most realistic definition of this little-known profession, which makes people smile most of the time, is :

"A person who intervenes between a man and a woman to bring them closer together, and facilitate the conclusion of a marriage."

This profession was imposed itself to her following the bitter observation about the attitude of some girls in her country and other countries of the African continent, forced to seek a better future by doing everything which is possible to find a fiance, then, a husband of European origin, and thus flee the misery to build a living environment a little more in adequacy with every girl's dream of being happy. Simply.

Who can blame them if we observe that, the life of those thousands of young girls who have no choice but to vegetate in their neighborhoods, living adventures without tomorrow with men reduced to their simplest expression by the grace of a very long-term unemployment, with no prospect of the future for most of them who otherwise , are unable to meet the obligations of man to meet his wife's most basic needs.

Thus, unsurprisingly, accidental pregnancies follow one another at a frantic pace, generating children at the chain, children who end up with grandparents (in the best case) or left to their own devices, condemned to wander and rub shoulders with the worst in the streets all day long, thus undermining their health and their future.

Heartbreaking for Fatoumata. Four of her nieces and nephews live at home, totally dependent on her.

From this observation, Fatoumata made the decision to change things. It's like to wanting to empty the sea with his teaspoon.

She likes to repeat the well-known phrase : "impossible is not French."

So, she went to war against what she considers to be an "eternal hemorrhage of the future", she deplores this future that disappears before existing.

Which is equivalent to the premature social death of all those young girls who dream of Charming Prince with all that goes with him.

How many of these young girls, (who were not born with a silver spoon in their mouths), can wait calmly for the arrival of this providential man worthy of the name, who can give them the bright future they dream of?

What events to satisfy what ambitions?

An european on holiday in a bush taxi ? A member of the diaspora on holiday in the country approached by the family? A little help from providence for a chance encounter in the street or on a beach?

What guarantee for them that this chance meeting on a beach or in an open-air bar, could lead to a serious relationship that could lead the two lovebirds in front of the mayor, allowing the departure towards the Eldorado so coveted?

How can we erase the disastrous image of these young girls in search of happiness, trying to make their way to the happiness that makes them so envious?

Tourists passing through or members of the diaspora back home facing these young girls with bright eyes of envy, all are in this false human relationship in which, everyone will try to make the most of the meeting to his / her exclusive benefit.

Sometimes Cupid forces fate. Everyone is happy and celebrating the happiness. They are preparing the journey to other heavens. At the airport, there are crying eyes, smiling lips. At the moment of goodbyes, joys mixed with sadness: a mother mourning the departure of her daughter, a little sister who smiles at the idea of being able to join the big sister very soon in Europe,..

Against all odds, this same Cupid sometimes ostensibly turns his head away, causing the most advanced plans of union to fail miserably, killing in the bud any prospect of the future.

So, once again, the heartbreak at the time of farewell : promises without a future in the lobby of the airport (Honey, I'll come back soon). Sometimes, for the most careless and the most oblivious by the current times with the AIDS, unexpected gifts left by visitors of whose they will never see them again.

Fatoumata's idea is simple : to force fate, even if the future in this matter, is not easy to manage.

She likes to repeat this thought of Dona Maurice ZANNOU to the young girls who come to ask her advice:

"There is no destiny all plotted. Forge yours by your perception, by your participation, by your determination and by your self-denial. »

In essence, she explains to them that the perception of this future they dream of should not be or remain something abstract.

Participating in the advent of this much desired happiness should require a fierce determination.

Anything that comes to life would be like the seed that begins to decompose in the earth before beginning its germination cycle.

In other words, without denying anything of the past or the socio-cultural environment to which they belong, they must be able to get rid of the adhesions (from this socio-cultural context) that have kept them until now in an emotional and economic dependence. For this could distort their perception and hinder their determination to adopt the right posture to achieve their life project.

At the head of an impressive network of neighborhood moms that allows her to spot the girls marriage candidate, Fatoumata has gradually built up a catalogue of potential brides.

Thanks to social networks and her stays in Europe, she engages in a methodical canvassing with the diaspora in an attempt to arouse the desire to meet the country's girls to marry.

She wants the country's girls to return towards the men of the country in priority.

For her, it can only be a source of stability, each understanding the other effortlessly mastering the habits and customs of the other, all this having to help create the ideal conditions for perfect cohesion within the future couple.

Personal notes

Personal notes

EDWIGE

In this late afternoon of March, in the stream of workers on the way to return home after (for most of them), a day of hard work, Edwige, twenty-six years old, piercing eyes, emerald green color, red hair, piercing to the left nostril, a multitude of bracelets on the wrists generating rattling at each of her steps as she advances.

Her profession: reader in a big publishing society.

Special sign: she tried three times to publish novels several years before she took office in the publishing house that employs her for three years.

Current state of mind: big frustration.

Sometimes the course of life unfolds in a disconcerting way.

Edwige, who believed for a moment (in her young life) to have written the manuscript of the novel of the year, and who saw her dreams as a well-known novelist, signing autographs in the book fairs, fly away, finds herself (by a curious coincidence) now in the position of the one who has the ability to make the rain and the good weather, to influence the destiny of future writers.

Having been rejected in her attempts to publish her manuscript, she had spent a great deal of time wishing the worst to the one who threw her manuscript to the nettles, thus depriving her of a supposed future glory.

Therefore, her questioning concerns the ability of a person who has never written a novel to stand up against the existence and recognition of sincere, arduous, useful work.

From this questioning, results her conviction that the position she holds in this publishing house, is legitimized by her knowledge of the mechanisms of writing which allows her to decide the publication or not of a novel.

She had sweated blood and water to make her writing project come to fruition.

She knows what the writer's trance is. She knows the pangs of the blank page. She felt in her time and often this beginning of discomfort when the body orders the writer to stop writing to feed herself/himself. She knows everything about the writer's state of mind from A to Z.

Yes !

But, nevertheless, doubt is allowed as to her objectivity in the performance of her role as a manuscript reader.

This doubt stems from the fact that the human soul cannot get rid of resentment so easily, resentment defining itself as the state of mind of who remembers with animosity the wrongs from which she/he has suffered. This generates an persistent pain that gnaws and obscures discernment.

Seen in this light, how could one logically believe that Miss Edwige could recommend a

FACES

manuscript which she would have read diagonally, and which she would have constantly compared to hers by denigrating it in her inner self, establishing herself as a supreme judge in this intimate court of her conscience, condemning (de facto) and without appeal the manuscripts that are deposited every morning on her desk?

How many good future writers have thus fallen through the cracks under the dictatorship of Miss Edwige, if they did not have the good idea to contact other publishing houses in parallel ?

Such a situation is eerily reminiscent of a conflict of interest.

Miss Edwige finds herself at the center of a decision each time where her objectivity and neutrality can be called into question, and would have cost to her, her position, if however, she failed to mention the successive rejections of her manuscript during her job interview.

It is more than likely that the position would

have eluded her if she had had the honesty to talk about it.

Who can blame her?

Who's to blame?

The HRD who has not been able to ask her the right questions for the purpose of probing her mind in her intellectual functioning?

Or she herself, who throughout these years in this position of reader, did not know or did not want to impose herself and observe this necessary distancing required by ethics involving the unfailing application of moral principles in the exercise of her function as reader?

Seen from the outside, does this jubilant censorship imposed by her in this unorthodox exercise of her profession, give her the certainty of doing useful work by rejecting the manuscripts of these aspiring novelists?

Useful work in what?

Probably in her mind perverted by an irrepressible desire for revenge, the certainty that the world of literature would be better off without those people who have the pretension to write novels and who, according to her, have no talent.

Make way for clean.

Preparing her advent in this very closed environment in which, there are so many called and few elected.

Personal notes

Personal notes

THIERRY

Paris, early December, 6 a.m.

It's cold. It's very cold. The air is freezing

Exhaust pipes of cars smoke. The warmly dressed passers on their way to work, hurry and rush into the subway mouths.

At the intersection of Turbigo Street and Réaumur Street, opposite the Arts et Métiers subway, the garbage truck makes a stop, forcing cars to move forward at the rate of garbage collection.

Behind, two garbage collectors jump from the steps located on either side of the truck. And in a ballet tuned to the millimeter, they grab the trash cans, cling them to the heaving device that is responsible for dumping them in the big garbage collection tank. Seconds later, the trash cans are deposited on the ground, freed from the articulated arms of the device, and the two garbage collectors reposition them in front of the buildings.

Classic scene of collecting household garbage.

So, so far, nothing special.

One of the two garbage collectors is named Thierry.

He is from Burgundy, more precisely from Dijon.

He is preparing a thesis in mechanical engineering and is expected to pass this thesis in front of a jury at the end of the academic year.

The logical next step : a teaching position to transmit his knowledge to the younger generation.

At a time when his classmates are almost all in offices, performing tasks deemed nobler and less messy, he chose to be a garbage collector in the city of Paris during this period when every student in need must find and perform a job generating a minimum wage to cover the daily expenses.

Thus, cashier during the weekend in a supermarket, night watchman with a dog on a construction site, or for the lucky ones, a position in the tertiary sector related to the activities of companies that will be able to keep them and integrate them into their workforce, once the diploma in hand, whatever the nature of the job, the main thing is to get a job to survive.

He, his daily life, is to take care of the waste produced by the society of men which, in a frantic race, consumes more and more and releases as much waste as it was possible to produce.

However, his parents live in a mansion in a wealthy part of the city, and are part of the local bourgeoisie.

Therefore, Thierry does not need this job to survive during his schooling.
He receives a bank check every month from

his parents to pay for his housing and remains discreet about his morning activities on the streets of Paris.

He returns once a month within his family and behaves like an "ordinary" doctoral student, discusses the progress of his thesis with his parents, both university professors.

His workmate, the other garbage collector who shares his rounds morning after morning behind the same garbage truck, do you remember? The one standing on the other step behind the truck, who is it?

Who is this person of African origin, the cap screwed on the head, unrecognizable behind the big protective glasses, agile and very skilful with the hands, who knows how to juggle with trash cans like no one can do it?

The name of person is Malika.

Occupation : Full-time garbage collector, registered in the accounting books of the city of Paris.

Special sign: boyish haircut.

Status: Thierry's girlfriend.

They live in the same neighbourhood in a Paris suburb and met fortuitously at the mall.

From this meeting a beautiful friendship was born that gradually turned into a great love story.

Malika didn't hesitate for a moment to talk to him about her job. She told him about it so well that Thierry (against all odds) felt attracted by this profession that some people would describe as a public utility but that many others would hesitate to practice.

 Practising a job because a relative has praised the thousand and one aspects of this profession, is not comparable to the attitude to adopt in front of a restaurant which is not attractive but of which dishes (as it seems) are succulent.

At worst, we enter out of curiosity and if the

reputation is not probative, we do not return to it.

In Thierry's case, being a garbage collector is like making a life choice, knowing that, every choice demands (or even requires) sacrifices.

Thierry may in this case have sacrificed his discernment and his freedom to act for the exclusive benefit of his love for Malika.

He could, by extension, mortgage his relationship with his parents in front of his choice of life, whose reality they will never accept.

His preferences, namely, being a garbage collector or doctor of mechanical engineering, to teach in front of students (who have nothing to do with his theories), are in balance with his convictions that awaken his consciousness and push him to be useful to society by collecting its garbage every morning.

If his passion for this profession lasts forever and in the future, his love for Malika keeps him in this state of exaltation in which he finds himself at the moment, how could he explain to his parents his 360-degree turn?

Perhaps his parents, at the time of the confrontation, will go through the different phases of denial, rejection, fear, anger, guilt. And what else do I know?

However, they may try to put their disappointment aside.

They will be able to try to accept the unacceptable and take a different view of what it is to choose one's life.

Then, end their role as parents in the choice of life of their child and thus allow the child to determine himself in order to conduct his own experiences in a sovereign way.

What is sure, only he can reap the rewards or disappointments of his experiences.

The role of parents is to provide the necessary tools to enable their child's success in the future.

But, how can they justified in pretending to know what is good or harmful for the future generation?

By vertue of their own experiences?

What father, what mother could claim to hold the patent for the best life experience to the point of wanting to change that of his/her child?

In the animal kingdom, from a certain age, the next generation cuts this invisible bond and assumes its own destiny.

The only remarkable element that remains after this necessary separation from the generation before, is what atavism commands to do or not to do. Things are extremely clear. The new generation pays cash for its mistakes. That's the way it is.

This atavism informs the new generation about how to deal with life.

And thanks to this wonderful and mysterious mode of transmission, successive generations perpetuate traditions and maintain their survival instincts.

It is easy to imagine the atmosphere that sets in during family lunches when the child who "denotes" (the one who does not observe the right dress code) arrives : shaved head, a twenty-day beard, holed jeans, scruffy outfit, masculine attitude adopted by the rebellious girl, piercing, etc. ... .

At best, the child will be looked down upon and at worst, ignored by all, to the great despair of his parents when the choice of his profession goes against the general tendency imagined and imposed by the them, on behalf of "what is good for the child".

Thus, the child who will evolve in the footsteps of his parents, will be considered a child-king, worthy of interest, sometimes adored, while the one who would be rebel, will just be tolerated. He cannot be brought back to the store for a standard exchange. Parents will have to deal with it, and will be sorry to have fathered a being that does not look like them.

They will blame each other, accusing each other of being the source of the defect that strikes the offspring.

What is certain, as far as one can go back in the line of Thierry, there has never been a garbage collector.

As for Malika's existence in Thierry's life, the role she played in getting into it, and the fact that she is at the very beginning of a happy event, it's another matter.

Personal notes

Personal notes

PASCALINE

In this corridor north of this important hospital in the centre of Bordeau, Professor A. Pascaline, surrounded by her interns, heads to the rooms to begin her daily visits according to the usual protocol.

She wears glasses mounted on a multicolored frame, making her face bright and somewhat funny.

Anyone who meets her in this hospital remembers her face.

Her physical appearance would almost make her look like an eccentric in a white blouse or a clown who came to distract sick children, if her presence in the austere section of cancerology, surrounded by her interns, did not contradict this first impression.

Indeed, Pascaline is far from an eccentric.

Pascaline is a reputable oncologist.

She is world-famous. The patients come from far away to consult her.

Her diagnoses are of a so-called surgical precision, her opinions are without appeal. A second opinion is generally not necessary after the statement of her verdict.

That's the way it is.

She is the author of countless publications about this disease, which she stalks all day long with a pugnacity that commands respect.

She's got an incredible flair. In the framework of her profession, she has a special knack for flushing out and taming the « crab ».

Her specialty : the brain cancer.

Her cancerology skills make her the most respected and adulated specialist in the medical community in her field of expertise.

For her, a day won over the disease is a

victory to be credited to the patient.

Her method to stimulate the combativeness of patients (among others), is to set at the beginning of treatment, a number of points to be reached within a given time, a number of points corresponding to a crutial step of treatment, a step announcing the next, and then the one that comes after until the final step leading to healing.

Her method works well, as long as patients adhere to it.

Medicine for her is more than a passion. She's tenacious. Her fights against this disease, of which she knows all the secrets, are legendary. Patients who sometimes arrive on stretchers, leave on their both legs. She commands the admiration of her colleagues.

What revolts her above all and leads her to transcend herself is to see the disease attacking children sometimes very young, helpless, knowing nothing about life.

Her beliefs in God are very limited, even if

from time to time she goes to meet the one she condemns when terminally ill young children are entrusted to her, to whom she nevertheless manages to give them back time to grow up a little, waiting for the new advances of medicine.

She does not believe in the existence of Karma, which strikes people who are beholden to life (it seems).

To those who say that an infant who has cancer would be indebted in his previous existence, and who, on returning to the world, will have to pay this karmic debt, she replies with a great anger :

N O N S E N S E !

Faced with such words and in front of distraught parents, she always takes the necessary time to explain what cancer is, thus demonstrating the gap that exists between a supposed karmic debt (if proven) and the anarchic proliferation of cells in the human body.

Despite her rational, rigorous and somewhat formalistic spirit, Professor A. Pascaline has a big secret.

One and only one person knows this secret, and this person lives thousands of kilometers from Bordeaux, exactly at 11,902.38 kilometers bird's-eye view.

Once a year, Pascaline travels this long road like a pilgrim. She looks forward to this moment, not to bathe in the Seas of China, Sulu, Java, but to see her old friend who lives on the banks of the Kinabatangan River, the old friend to whom she saved his life in Bordeaux.

Yes you guessed : Pascaline goes to Borneo every year.

Once there, she must endure each time this humid environment, this stifling atmosphere, this mesmerizing place. A hostile place for a delicate European woman and wearing multicolored glasses.

But what she comes to do there with her old

friend, is beyond comprehension.

Indeed, the faculty of medicine would see very badly what she comes to do there, given her status as a world famous oncologist.

The old friend, was formerly a medicine professor. He was Pascaline's thesis director, and was impressed by the skills of this extremely gifted doctoral student to whom he had entrusted his fate later when he has been diagnosed a rare cancer.

After a fierce battle with her mentor's cancer, Pascaline finally found the right protocol, allowing total remission after months of treatment.

The cause was desperate.

The hope of recovery, almost no-existent.

Yet she had achieved this spectacular result, definitively sealing this great friendship between her mentor and her, she the little doctor with multicolored glasses, in front of this giant of medicine who possesses an encyclopedic knowledge of medicine.

During the research and development of this protocol, against all odds, Pascaline had agreed to follow the instructions of her mentor, (originally from Borneo and in the utmost secrecy, a follower of this decried medicine, called "traditional", practiced on her native island).

His instructions had led to observe spectacular advances that led to his accelerated healing.

It was troubling for her that the responses to the treatments of so-called "modern" medicine were not satisfying, whereas the application of the protocol derived from traditional medicine (a combination of carefully chosen plants) had caused a notorious change that triggered the healing process.

Day after day, blood tests, various clinical examinations confirmed the regression of the cancer, and the health of the patient got better and better until his final recovery. Regular post-treatment checks also confirmed this finding, and subsequently the declaration of the remission.

Faced with such obviousness, Pascaline could not bring herself to accept what she experienced by putting herself (at the request of her mentor who had nothing to lose), outlawed. It is not permissible to apply a protocol that has not been certified by health authorities. As a result, Pascaline was complicit in a serious misconduct that could lead her in front of the Medical Council. But the only person who could denounce her is her teacher, in front of whom she had defended her thesis, and to whom she saved his life by following his instructions.

Her trouble is real in the face of this situation in which her fidelity to her oath to save lives, runs up against the method used to save this particular patient.

"The end justifies the means," says the old saying.

So, is it possible that in medicine, a doctor (who has taken the oath) may be willing to use reprehensible means (with regard to so-called modern medicine) to obtain the patient's recovery, no matter what ?

As a result, will healing have to be justified to excuse the method?

This questioning cost her sleepless nights.

In the end, unable to take advice from anyone, she decided to pursue this parallel path to see where it would lead her.

Of course she doesn't think about the Nobel Prize, but a few lives saved would justify endangering her career.

This is the starting point of her interest in traditional medicine for which she takes this trip every year to Borneo.

Personal notes

Personal notes

LARA

Lara took a day off for personal reasons.

Very personal reasons indeed. She comes out of a visit to her gynecologist.

She's distraught.

She's pregnant.

The result of a moment of weakness, during an outing with colleagues from the police station.

Lara's a police officer.

Policewoman, not out of vocation, but because before her, her father and grandfather were high-ranking police officers.

She is an only child, and had no choice despite her gender and her mother's reluctance to join this predominantly male institution.

Lara does not have a real attraction for this profession that she did not choose, but which she nevertheless exercises with courage and respect.

She would have wanted to travel in the world, discover new civilizations, write books, paint landscapes on her easel installed in the wild, find a stable house, live in a big house, full of children.

But instead, she lives a dangerous life punctuated with the exercise of authority, (which she hates above all else), an uncertain life (a well-started day does not guarantee a quiet end of the day), and finally, the obligation to hide her femininity behind the wearing of the uniform, (she who loves to put herself to her advantage, she so delicate).

She is in the right period of her life as a woman where her body allows her to have one or more pregnancies without problem.

Therefore, getting pregnant (even in the

conditions in which it happened) can only be a source of happiness, as further regularization (with the future dad) is always possible.

But, (there is a big "BUT"), it is also the period when she is engaged in a process of career development within her unit at the police station (the examination including at least a sports test), in perfect contradiction with the outcome of her pregnancy. Indeed, she is fully prepared for the internal competitions for her advancement in accordance with the career plan planned and followed by her father.

Big dilemma: her baby, right now, putting a brake on the evolution of his career, or, priority, a career in pure respect of family tradition?

Against all odds, the confirmation of her pregnancy has triggered an awareness in her that she is missing out on her life.

Indeed, how can one admit to practising the profession of our ascendants by proxy?

Why should she add her best years to those (beautiful and long) that allowed her grandfather and father to pursue a busy career in their time and to ignore her own destiny?

She suddenly became aware of this cumbersome heritage, weighed down by the weight of tradition, tradition she doesn't want to care about anymore.

She refuses to continue to be a link in this chain of ancestral interdependence which, until this very moment, has guided and weighed on her existence.

She refuses to mortgage the realization and future of her own aspirations.

Her desire for liberation is strong.

She doesn't want to sacrifice her baby.

To do this, she needs to cut this invisible bond forged by her father and grandfather who keeps her in this police station against her will, cutting this cord that prevents her from evolving and living her own life.

She knows in advance the consequences of this renouncement to pursue her career according to the plan set out by her father.

She guesses the disappointment of her dad who prepared her all these years to make an exemplary career in the police.

She is not sure that she can count on the unwavering support of her mother, who, by marrying her father, had also married the police institution.

If, to this day, she has never objected to her husband's choices towards her daughter, how could she approve and support her daughter's decision to stop living her father's life by proxy?

She perceives in advance, relational tensions within the family, mainly between Lara and her father.

The peace and harmony that have prevailed within the family are in danger of breaking down. She would not want to experience such a situation to have to face the quasi-military

73   *FACES*

character of a person in the shadow of whom she has lived so far without ever daring to challenge any of his decisions.

It is not even certain that she is able to understand her daughter who wants to wear dresses and not a police uniform, her daughter who would like to establish gentle relationships with those around her, and not be in a permanent power relationship with her fellow citizens.

More serious: would she be able to accept, to welcome and to love the baby of discord?

Personal notes

Personal notes

LUCY

Boarding room Roissy Charles de Gaulle airport.

Destination Rome.

Lucy, a jewelry designer, sits among the passengers departing for Italy.

She travels once a month to Italy to stock up on precious stones in Murano.

But this journey, which she is about to have, has a special character.

She had a hard time setting the date of her departure.

She's apprehensive about her return to Italy. She is all the more apprehensive about the response to the ultimatum she has issued to this man, who she would like to force to do what he cannot do, what bothers her a lot.

She's tenacious. She wants to go to the end of this madness that morality denies. But there is no rational answer to her madness.

Practicing Catholic, it was during a mass in the middle of the day in a neighbourhood chapel in Murano that she met Brother Carlo, parish priest.

The forties, slender look, the keen look, the soothing and reassuring voice.

A priest for about fifteen years, Brother Carlo is esteemed by his superiors. His homilies are very well attended and are far from boring. He is part of this new generation of religious who want to bring some modernity to the exercise of their mission as apostles of Christ.

During her previous visits to Murano, Lucy never failed to attend the noon Masses that became important moments in her life.

Gradually, a true friendship has developed between Brother Carlo and this woman

FACES

always sitting in the front row, on the tongue of whom, the priest delicately deposits the body of Christ by uttering the ritual sentence. He could almost smell her perfume, observe the features of her face, capture the thousand and one messages delivered by her eyes.

From the spiritual guide, Brother Carlo became a very close friend.

And against all odds, Lucy gave birth to a little Carla whose she attributes paternity to Brother Carlo.

He does not know his alleged daughter, now three years old.

Carla never made the trip to Italy with her mother. She should be on this last trip, but Lucy first wanted to settle an important detail with her alleged father, namely to get from him, agreement to bring him back to France and organize their union in the utmost secrecy.

She wants to marry the man who disguised himself as a priest.

She would like to unite with a man like no other. A man of the church, at least what is left of him insofar as, having taken the step by breaking his vow of chastity several times, he continues to hide behind his status as a priest which gives him a certain respectability of which Lucy has nothing to do.

In Lucy's eyes, his cassock is no longer an obstacle to overcome.

"If the obstacle is too high, don't persist in jumping over it, but just bypass it." says an old saying.

Lucy has understood the principle so well, to the point of succeeding in overcoming this obstacle without forcing herself too much.

However, she does not consider herself a heroine. She doesn't feel like a heroine. Nor she does consider herself like the last of the whores, the one who succeeded in suborning the servant of God, dressed with his cassock.

She considers herself like the one who hates this invisible rival who is pompously called "the son of God" against whom she has no hold.

She considers herself to be the one who has managed to thwart the vigilance of a man reputedly "pious" who has promised to dedicate his body and mind to the service of his religion.

During the moments of capitulation of this man disguised as a priest, Lucy, (cuddly and triumphant, deploying all her zeal to prevent her lover from showing any resistance, by trying to make him forget his vow to keep his body chaste and pure), almost has never managed to divert her gaze from the black cassock, this priestly attribute delicately placed on a chair next to the bed during his night visits.

This priest so called, at the moment of withdrawing, (probably to go to flog himself) takes with him, a spirit "troubled", fogged, filled with doubts.

But on the other hand, it's assumed that he is probably persuaded that, having the courage to wear again this black cassock, could spontaneously absolve him of his sin and thus, give him back that authority momentarily abandoned at the door when he surreptitiously enters Lucy's room, night after night.

For her and in every respect, this cassock is a permanent reminder of her determination to love this man to whom she gave herself, just as he who, in his time, knew how to give himself to Christ, on behalf of the same feeling of love that had deviated him from the path taken by these "ordinary" beings, those who did not receive this call (from God) so feared or hoped by some persons.

This cassock, which to itself only, symbolizes, at the same time, what's more sacred and what's more detestable (the silent presence which accuses), is the silent witness of those moments when, the demonic takes advantage over the divine, where, madness is stronger than reason.

For Lucy, what characterizes an ordained priest is his propensity to believe himself apart, that is to say, to believe that by being a man of flesh and blood like all other men of flesh and blood, he enjoys (in addition to his corruptible human nature), a pseudo superiority conferred on him by his vow of chastity, which prevents him from marrying , and that would make him virtuous.

Where does virtue end? Where does chastity begin?
Where does chastity end? Where does virtue begin?

Could the nobility of one overshadow the immortality of the other?

Would Brother Carlo try to make rhyme "chastity" with "cowardice" by attempting to project on Lucy, the obvious personal responsibility that he stubbornly refuses, definitively to assume ?

Lucy wonders.

What she does not understand and does not want to understand is the basis of a situation that goes beyond her understanding and reminds her strangely the deplorable one of the situation of the enterprise in which the internal regulation is more restrictive than the LAW.

How can this be?

How can we continue to maintain on pedestal a religious who, in the exercise of his mission, is reputed to be an exceptional creature since he is the chosen one of this supreme God, who has received his call to serve him, whereas in his personal life, this chosen one of God is the perfect illustration of what is the illusion?

How can there be double standards in the face of the requirement of probity induced by the interpretation of the dogma of religion and imposed by the church since the dawn of time?

How can one believe in the incorruptibility of the MAN (human being) operating in an environment in which the rule must be the freedom to exist or not to exist, to believe or not to believe, to respect the word given or to fail to respect our commitments?

In fact, didn't the human being invent free will, in order to relinquish his responsibilities in the face of his turpitudes? And to take into account that ability of the human being to freely self-determine, to think and commit acts, as opposed to the determinism that would be inscribed in the DNA of every human being allowing him to act in accordance with his own impulses?

Who decreed that the priest was a virtuous man?

What's the deep meaning of vow of chastity?

Why do pastors marry and priests not?

Why should Christ have the right to preempt the hearts of men to marry?

Why ? Why ? Why ?

Despite her questioning, her pride as a woman commands her to ignore the serious consequences of her past and present acts, which she fully assumes.

Carla is a reality.

Brother Carlo is a reality.

He is the man, the priest, the one who she said has contributed to the birth of her daughter Carla, no offense to the church.

She is determined to see her future in a radiant way, just like her expectation: brother Carlo, Carla and her, together in France in the most complete anonymity.

Personal notes

Personal notes

MERYEM

Far from her native Turkey, Meryem has been living in France for a few weeks.

She has just had lunch in the Halles district and walks around St Eustache Church, lingering in the modern Nelson Mandela garden.

She lives in Antalya where she owns a shoe store on the Riviera. A successful business. Guests (mainly wealthy tourists) flock in front of the store displays, presenting models of luxury shoes, and do not hesitate to enter into the shop.

Meryem is a single woman, elegant, rich and very courted.

Meryem's parents come from a very pious family, very attached to the values prescribed by their religion.

She is the free electron of the family, because of her positions, her style of dress, her way of life, ... It's a real desolation for her mother.

She loves to drink vintage champagne and taste all the good things that go with it.She loves life, the beautiful life and she doesn't deny herself anything. She travels the world for commercial purposes, and for her own pleasure.

Despite her apparent life without a shadow on the board, Meryem is experiencing a real drama.

For more than a year, she has been concerned about a problem of which, she does not see the end.

Her highest-ranking relations in her country have been involved, to no avail. She spent a lot of money without counting, to no avail.

So, her store put in management, she leaves Turkey to try to solve the problem herself.

A few weeks before arriving in France, she

was in Switzerland in the canton of Geneva in the footsteps of this passing lover who holds intimate pictures of her.

These pics are not so terrible compared to what one might imagine. Today, what does a pic showing a woman's breasts represent?

Nothing, because of the unbridled mores of today's society. In summer, the beaches are full of topless, and no one complains.

What upsets her and puts her out of her is the betrayal that her lover has committed towards her, by taking these pictures without her knowledge.

Betrayal on the part of a man with an angelic face, to whom she has devoted time, to whom she gave food, to whom she found work, to whom she filled the pockets, he, who was without a future, the man she almost has loved.

What motivates her above all to embark on this crusade, is her fear of having to face one day the reaction of her parents who would discover these pics. She fears the upheaval that will result from the publication of her pics on which, her face will be associated to a topless woman. She is afraid of losing the love of her parents forever , love already put to the test by her way of life.

It could kill her mother, as she keeps saying.

Once a month, she receives a letter containing a different photo on the back of which these words "Western Union" are written, followed by the name of a city.

In other words, she had to understand: I am in such a city in a particular country, send me money urgently.

The penultimate time, the city was Geneva. Now, Paris.

Thus, she follows in the footsteps of this evil lover as he moves, playing naively the detective, in the hope of finding this person who is disrupting her nights since several months.

She has her plan and hopes to achieve it very soon.

"*Resisting blackmail requires great strength both in the face of despair and self love.*"

How can Meryem resist this deep affliction?

Affliction as a double-sided mirror, namely, the one she is trying to overcome and the one caused by her misadventure, which could, if necessary, violently heurt the soul of her parents.

A fleeting pleasure (at the moment when she was spinning the perfect love with this passing lover that she exhibited everywhere like a trophy), who gradually became this displeasure that makes her shudder with disgust.

How can she continue to look at herself in this mirror that sends back the image of this woman who has lost (through this ordeal) her self love and by extension, her desire to live?

Personal notes

Personal notes

AHMED

Thirty-five years, married, school teacher, native of North Africa, five years of experience.

A belated vocation following an inner revolt which, in all its nobility, has generated over time, this desire to be part of those who make children want to learn.

But as far as he is concerned, this desire goes far beyond his desire to be the one who puts himself at the service of children to help them to structure their thinking and personality. He wants to create the ideal conditions for a perfect success for the future of these children in his care.

To learn the basics of knowledge according to the precepts a thousand and one times teached by generations of teachers in the schools of the republic, does not seem to him to

96

correspond to the purpose of this teaching which vocation is to train future citizens to live in a society in full decay.

His inner revolt was born as a result of the tragic events which shook the entire country.

Many voices have been raised to condemn and prescribe solutions. Solutions that deal downstream with the consequences of a situation instead of addressing its causes upstream. Solutions at the opposite end of the challenges facing society, he believes.

His questioning is simple and complex at the same time : how to make of a diversity at the beginning, a homogeneous mix on arrival?

How can we achieve this without seeming to be a pretentious utopian, the very one who asserts loud and clear that change must find its foundation in the early years of the life of the next generation ?

A new generation implies, in essence, the advent of a better world based on values once known but forgotten or set aside to make way for the various political ideologies which telescopes. As a result, the new generation is preparing to face an unsuitable world in which the most innocuous gestures can lead to the most unexpected consequences, likely to make headlines.

Nowadays, a school teacher (male or female) can no longer take a child in his/her arms to comfort him when that child is hurting himself as it was done in this not so distant time.

This simple, natural and spontaneous gesture has a special character that could harm its author in the present day.

So, if at this level things are already so complicated for the one whose mission is to take charge of the first steps of this new generation, how to do when, in the world to come, comes to graft what is left of our civilization more than decadent, "weighed down" with memories of the wrongs suffered by the previous generation , especially when these memories lead to uncontrolled anger, rage facing the impotence to act, causing extremist actions occasioning irreversible damage and trauma among the innocent population which is not at all concerned?

Having said that, taking this issue into account, how does Mr Hamed, the school teacher , the one who wants to make his contribution to the building by trying to change the world, how does he see things? What is his room for manoeuvre?

In short, freeing souls from the resentment conveyed by atavism.

Vast program indeed.

Let's try to make it a little clearer.

Apart from the strict program set out by the Ministry of National Education in the care of primary school children, the fact remains that the school teacher is not intended to wear the clothes of the atavistic eraser, an area not listed in the disciplines taught in normal schools.

Mr. Hamed could skew by using the daily

hour dedicated to the moral lesson to spread the messages aimed at sowing the seeds that must germinate in the brains of the children in his care from year to year, and lead them to adopt the right attitude towards the phenomena that may trigger in them, predictable revolts, which can lead to the achievement of wrongdoing and harmful acts to society which aspires only to live in peace.

How could he combat the perverse effects of collective memory maintained from generation to generation?

How can these young souls learn to identify and defuse angry situations?

Who remembers the wise or not advice of a teacher received at an early age?

The child who has become a man or a woman, living and evolving in an environment in which the stigmata of ancestral bullying, are a constant reminder to maintain the revolt at the service and benefit of the community.

This excludes any intellectual approach to finely analyzing situations in which resentment is exacerbated by calls for revenge to be worthy of belonging to that community.

Therefore, how could Mr Hamed imagine for a moment holding the secret to put an end to intergenerational revolts in the society of MEN, a society in which the supposed benefits of social diversity are a pure illusion?

Personal notes

Personal notes

In the end ...

The world of all these people we meet, has something to surprise us pleasantly or sometimes, in a disconcerting way.

A face, a look, an attitude, all contribute to invite us to imagine what is behind, not to look through the keyhole, but to prolong the encounter that we   have just made and which lasted a few seconds.

Such a short time, or considered as such, is more than enough to transform our vision of what surrounds us.

Our mind opens up and our imagination takes the lead.

Our journey becomes less monotonous. We become the privileged witnesses of slices of life until then, away from prying eyes.

FACES

A singular indiscretion on my part, indeed.

You will no longer see the people you meet on your journey in the same way in the future.

If so, my happiness will be total.

I have taken infinite pleasure in inviting you to be by my side during these imaginary encounters which will have raised I am sure, many questions for which your sagacity will provide us with the appropriate answers which, I'm sure, will instruct us.

Thanks.

END.

FACES
© *Nathanaël AMAH , 2020   NATHAM Collection*

FACES

Éditeur : BoD-Books on Demand, 12/14 rond point des Champs Élysées, 75008 Paris, France
Impression: BoD-Books on Demand, Norderstedt, Allemagne
ISBN : **9782322257140**
Dépôt légal : November, 2020

FACES